POP THE CORN

by Ellen Appelbaum
illustrated by Wallace E. Keller

Orlando   Boston   Dallas   Chicago   San Diego

Visit *The Learning Site!*

www.harcourtschool.com

Mom calls Jon.
Where is Jon?

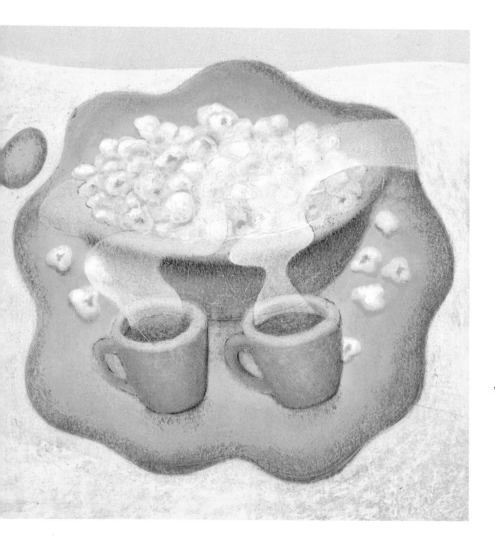

Jon wants popcorn.
Did Mom buy corn
to pop?

3

Here is a pot.
They pop all of
the corn.

4

Jon calls Mom.
All the corn falls.

That is a lot of corn!
It is in a very tall
bag.

Mom makes balls.
Jon wants to help.

That is where
the balls can go.